THE
SECRETARIAL
SHELTER

Also by Alexandria Blaelock

SHORT STORY COLLECTIONS
The Histories of Hayward Hall
Lovelorn, Lovestruck and Love at First Sight
Common or Garden Variety Heroes
Case Files of the Wilkinson Detective Agency
Unavoidable Fates
Christmas Travesties
Five Faces of Felicia Clarke
Little Place Called Home
Security Directorate Dossiers v. 1.
Security Directorate Dossiers v. 2.

FICTION
That Love Nonsense
Taipan vs Brown
The Ghost and Ms Cox
Friends Like That
Weaving the Wildwood
Wolf vs Orb

MS BLAELOCK'S BOOKS
Stress Free Dinner Parties
Signature Wardrobe Planning
Holistic Personal Finance
Minimally Viable Housekeeping
Planning a Life Worth Living

PICTURE BOOKS
Australia Felix

SELECTED SHORT STORIES
Alma's Grace
Blood and Bloody Profanity
Cancelled by the Cartel
Dingo Hunting
Honoris Virilis Respectu
Mince Pie Mystery
Remains of Christmas

THE SECRETARIAL SHELTER

A FELICIA CLARKE
SHORT STORY

ALEXANDRIA BLAELOCK

BlueMere Books
MELBOURNE, AUSTRALIA

Ordering Information:
Discounts are available on quantity purchases. For details, contact orders@bluemerebooks.com.

The Secretarial ShelterAlexandria Blaelock
paperback ISBN: 978-1-922744-10-4
digital ISBN: 978-1-922744-11-1

Book Layout © BookDesignTemplates.com
Cover Art © Stevica Mrda via depositphotos

THE SECRETARIAL SHELTER

When Mr Charles Weatherby of Weatherby & Sons, Inc. first met Miss Felicia Clarke he was impressed by her self-possession.

Sitting in his office, calm, composed and controlled in the hard chair on the other side of his overly large, inherited mahogany desk.

Back straight, hands folded quietly in her lap.

She'd tucked her small bag under the chair as she'd sat down, and it wasn't quite concealed by the fall of her old-fashioned long skirt.

She did not move without purpose during the entire time she was there.

Not a fidget, nor a gesture, not even to uncross and recross her legs.

Not once.

When he thought back, he wasn't entirely convinced she'd even blinked.

Miss Clarke had been referred to him by his good friend Barnaby who thought she might do well as young Mr Sutton's first secretary.

Barnaby was retiring at the end of the year, and he was determined to see his secretary placed somewhere appropriate before he closed his practice.

He couldn't recommend her highly enough and had spoken warmly of her calm competence on more than one occasion.

And of the duplicitous charm she could switch on and off as the situation warranted, such that she'd had the famously brutish industrialist John Sumner eating out of her hand.

A delight to behold Barnaby had said.

Such a shame about her fiancé; dead of tetanus. Very nasty business.

Seemingly, never so much as looked at another man.

Not that anyone was going to want to marry a woman her age, but nonetheless, her status as a dried-up spinster made her more reliable than the young, flighty women who were just looking to marry a lawyer.

But the thing about Miss Clarke that intrigued him the most, was that she watched him watching her.

Like a barn cat honing in, ready to pounce on an unsuspecting small bird or mouse.

She appeared to be assessing his suitability as an employer, and he had the oddest feeling he was disappointing her.

And if she didn't like him, she would refuse his offer of employment, no matter what the capacity.

Somewhat disconcerting that he felt she found him remarkably lacking in some way.

He had of course attempted to bully and hector all the candidates; in the legal profession a secretary is bound to come across many distressed and unhappy clients, and Charles considered it an essential part of a secretary's role to shelter the lawyer in question.

And he had no doubt Mr Sutton would result in many aggrieved parties arriving at her desk.

However, given that her expressionless face and steady gaze was making a man of his age and experience feel like a callow youth, he didn't doubt she would be a formidable barrier to any disgruntled client.

Charles had no idea how long she'd been waiting in reception before she'd reported herself.

She'd arrived so discreetly his own secretary Butler hadn't seen her arrive, so she'd seen at least one young woman depart in tears.

Butler was old school, one of the last of the male secretaries. Didn't in principle approve of women in the office.

Not proper as far as he was concerned.

Perversely, the cooler Miss Clarke's reception, the more Charles was convinced of her suitability.

Butler knocked on the closed door of the office, barely pausing before walking in, carrying a cup of fragrant Earl Grey tea by the saucer to his desk and departing with a sniff.

The shortbread biscuit Charles permitted himself at three o'clock slipped from the saucer to the blotting paper covered desk with a small thud that seemed to reverberate around the room.

Miss Clarke smiled slightly and raised one eyebrow, but otherwise remained still.

Charles almost started to make excuses before remembering who, and where he was.

Besides, he couldn't tell whether she was smiling at his afternoon tea, or the fact she hadn't been offered any.

Miss Clarke was obviously a force to be reckoned with, she'd be wasted on Mr Sutton.

Had she been like that when she was engaged?

A terrifying prospect making him pity the man she as engaged to.

She looked at the overly large man's wristwatch swamping her delicate wrist, then folded herself in half to pick up her bag and stand up in one smooth movement, "if there's nothing further?"

He had to concede there was not, and nodding, "I expect to make a decision shortly, you can expect a letter by the end of next week."

"Then I'll bid you a good day Mr Weatherby," and she was gone.

Not in a lingering haze of strong perfume as the candidate preceding her, after whom they'd had to open and close the windows several times to clear the air.

No doubt he'd need to air his suit thoroughly before he wore it again.

But such was the speed of Miss Clarke's exit, he could have sworn there was a small pop as the displaced air left the loose papers on his desk flapping in her wake.

«« • »»

Charles struggled through another two interviews before the last candidate left squalling, and it was safe to say they suffered by comparison to Miss Clarke.

All the candidates suffered by comparison to Miss Clarke.

Charles was at a complete loss, not a situation that he was accustomed to.

Butler returned to take Charles' cold tea away.

Surely one secretary could size the others up, why not ask his own for an opinion?

"Stay a minute Butler," he said indicating the chair, "tell me what you think of the candidates."

Butler sat on the edge of the hard chair, shoulders up around his head, and cleared his throat.

Then said nothing.

He swallowed, Adam's apple bouncing, and cleared his throat again, "you recall my son moved to Manchester to take up a clerking position in a cotton factory?"

"Yes of course, how is he doing?"

"Doing well Sir. Got married, and we just heard they're pregnant."

"That's excellent news, congratulations."

Charles was starting to get an idea of where the conversation was heading.

"Um... Mrs Butler wants to move up there to be nearby, and... Er..."

"She wants you to resign and go too?"

Butler's shoulders dropped as if he was glad to have it out in the open at last, "ah... Yes Sir."

"I see. And I can't persuade you to stay?"

Butler shrugged, "you know what they say Sir, happy wife happy life."

"I see," though never having been married, Charles didn't see at all.

"So the way I see it, the only one of them's any good is the quiet one, Miss Clarke, and she's too good for Sutton.

"You should hire her for yourself, and the young one..." he looked up at the ceiling struggling to re-member the name, "Miss Evans for Mr Sutton; the two young'uns can muddle through together.

"Miss Clarke ought to be able to help Miss Ev-ans get through some of it, the rest she'll have to learn on her own."

"This coming from the man who doesn't think women belong in offices?"

Butler sighed. "My wife tells me I should move with the times, but I'm not sure I want to. Man-chester is more conservative, so I think I'll do well there."

"I understand," though to be honest, Charles didn't have a frame of reference for that either.

«« • »»

It wasn't that Charles was selfish or self-involved, just that he tended to get caught up in the cases he was working on.

And so it came as somewhat of a surprise to find that Butler had gone and Miss Clarke had more or less seamlessly taken over his duties.

"I should have sent him away with something," Charles fretted.

"You did, you gave him a gold watch."

"Did I? Surely I would remember if I had."

"You were buried in the Sweet case at the time, so given his loyalty and length of service, I purchased the watch and had it engraved on your behalf."

Charles stood up and blustered, "I should have been consulted."

Miss Clarke sat down, "you were. Do you not recall I offered you the catalogue to choose? And asked what sentiment the engraving should be?"

"I—

"Ah... Yes... I apologise.

"Is it not very odd he didn't thank me?"

She stood up to rifle through the top layers of papers on his desk for Butler's letter, "it's here. I'll bring you some tea and leave you to read it."

He sat heavily in his chair, raised the letter to look at it, and thought how awfully he seemed to have behaved.

Miss Clarke returned with his tea, and this time two biscuits, seeming to understand he needed a little extra something.

Charles read the letter, somewhat reassured to find Butler had only just left.

That he appreciated the minimum of fuss, not being one to socialise with the lower employees.

And had appreciated the watch and the warmth of the gesture, and would always treasure it.

Charles sighed.

Then put his coat and hat on, telling Miss Clarke he was going for a walk.

"I've freed your afternoon, so don't feel obliged to return," she said.

So he didn't.

«« • »»

He found a subtle difference to the offices when he returned the next day.

As if someone had opened all the windows to let some fresh air in.

And cleaned them all to let more light in too.

Miss Clarke had installed some kind of yellow flowers on her desk and they certainly brightened up the place.

She gave him a moment to remove his hat and coat, and reorient himself before bringing in a tray with two cups of tea, thereby giving him to understand they were playing by her rules from now on.

He signed some letters and orders, they talked through some matters she could progress, and she laid out his schedule for the day.

As he looked past her and out the window onto a dreary day, he noticed a jug of water and four glasses on the credenza by the window, and wondered why he hadn't thought of that before.

A little later, when she ushered his first appointment in, he offered them some water and she winked at him.

And a little later, with another client, she brought a tea tray with a pot of tea and two cups by which he understood that this client needed a little more time and attention.

On another occasion, there was even a plate of biscuits to accompany the tea.

He understood her level of client care was a clue, guiding him towards his next action.

Not to say that she was anything other than professional, but as Barnaby had suggested, she was able to chop and change her approach according to what each client needed.

And so, as a little thank you, he started bringing her flowers on Monday mornings.

Just a small token bunch at first, but as the years progressed, the more elaborate the arrangements became, until after many more years it became necessary to acquire a dedicated table to sit them on.

Every Friday evening, Miss Clark donated the flowers somewhere or another; Charles told himself it was not appropriate to question her on the issue.

But the truth was, he was a little afraid to; better she donate them than throw them in the bin.

Over time, it became clear that she could get to the heart of a matter - very often what clients said was not the issue at all.

As if a doctor, she saw through the symptoms to the cause, and generally by the time someone came pursuing legal solutions, there were a lot of symptoms.

That's not to say that she knew the Law intimately, more that she understood people, and would often lead him down previously unexplored avenues of inquiry.

He started to get a reputation of case resolution *before* court proceedings commenced, and correspondingly, more clients who paid their less expensive bills more promptly.

Charles took to offering her a little sherry at the end of each week to celebrate their successes.

And it wasn't much later she relaxed enough to suggest he could call her Felicia outside of office hours.

And of course, he asked her to call him Charles.

There is no doubt that over time, the relationship between secretary and employer can be intimate.

People don't snigger about "the wife at the office" for no reason.

And very often a man spends more time at work with his secretary than he does at home with his wife.

Especially where there are rambunctious children at home too.

There is a kind of forced familiarity, an unintentional confidentiality that comes about *because* they spend so much time together.

This intensity can easily be confused for love.

And so it was for Charles.

He'd been working closely with Miss Clarke for many years when he attempted to kiss her after too many sherries one Friday evening.

«« • »»

It's tempting to say that Miss Clarke returned his affection, that they got married and lived Happy Ever After.

I know you, dear reader, would like that, and would possibly feel much more satisfied if I did.

But Real Life isn't like the kind of Fairy Stories we tell little girls hoping they'll grow up to be empty-headed and biddable beauties.

Real Life requires ongoing calculation and assessment of your options.

Would Miss Clarke be better off surrendering her independence and marrying some guy?

Could he possibly take better care of her than she could herself?

Was her resting bitch face a better deterrent than the threat of an irate husband?

That's not to say that Miss Clarke wasn't tempted now and then, but the more you keep your own company, the less you want to share it.

Happy Ever After doesn't take account of washing your husband's stinky socks and underpants.

Nor his coming home drunk again, passing out on the doorstep leaving you to manhandle him up the stairs and into your bed.

That he expects you to keep to his schedule, showing no regard to your own.

So when your own Fairy Tale presents itself to you, consider whether you might be falling for the propaganda.

Think about the downsides as well as the up.

«« • »»

So poor Charles had, after too many sherries, attempted to kiss Felicia one Friday evening.

Luckily, he hadn't had so many sherries he didn't detect her sudden rigidity.

And came to the uncomfortable truth that he had misconstrued their familiarity for love.

And in that instant, he weighed up his options; a task men seem more able for.

He now knew marriage was not one of them.

He was greatly tempted to ignore the situation; pretend it had never happened.

But he correctly thought if he didn't acknowledge his transgression, he would never see her again.

These calculations took mere fractions of a second.

Mortified, he let her go as he stumbled back.

"I was out of line," he blurted, "I apologise. It won't happen again."

She stood up, placing her glass on his desk, and examining his face at great length.

For such a long time he was worried he'd be frozen in place forever.

Seemingly satisfied, she said, "then I forgive you," and left the room.

As he put a hand on his heart, attempting to slow its pace, he heard her collect her things and leave.

He sat heavily in his chair, hoping she wasn't the kind of woman who held grudges, though he'd never had an inkling she might be.

Charles fretted all weekend.

«« • »»

Monday morning arrived, and he bought a simple bunch of carnations into the office because he knew they were his favourite flower.

As usual, she thanked him, and gave him a moment to remove his hat and coat before she brought in the tea tray.

And as usual, they discussed his schedule, other related matters and he signed the letters and orders.

As she collected the papers together, he cleared his throat and said, "about Friday—"

"There's no need to say another word, it's as forgotten as if it never happened."

And true to her word, it really was as if it had never happened.

So much so, that many years after that, when he took the memory out and looked at it, it seemed like the fevered dream of his over-active imagination.

«« • »»

When at last Charles retired, he, like Barnaby all those years ago, fretted about what to do with Felicia.

And tried to shop her around to his friends in the legal profession, but time had moved on.

She had no qualifications, wasn't fond of type-writers that moved faster than her, and not completely sure about those new-fangled computers.

He broached the subject with her, and she surprised him.

She would retire herself.

Take trips to visit her sisters in New Zealand and Australia.

Do all those other things she'd been waiting for the available time to do.

«« • »»

Their last day together passed uneventfully.

It wasn't much more than a formality.

All the files were fully written up and dispatched to their new owners.

His office was clean and empty, ready for its new owner.

They took one last long lunch, at the end of which she shook his hand and walked away.

Charles Weatherby never saw Felicia Clark again, but often wondered how she was faring.

THE END

As a small token of my thanks for reading...

Please enjoy 10% off everything (excluding shipping)

at alexandriablaelock.com

with the code weatherbyten.

Turn the page for some ideas where to use it,

Do you have what it takes to be a hero?

Whether that's running into a burning building, standing up for what you know is right, or saving the Princess it's going to take everything you've got and more besides.

In this genre-spanning collection of original stories, five women draw on resources they didn't know they had.

Join them, if you dare.

Home is where the heart is

You can struggle to find the place you call home. It's not a place, it's a feeling. You'll know it when you find it.

This collection of short stories explores our search for a place we can call home.

Short, sweet and relatable, these stories will make you homesick for places you've never been.

Welcome to Wilkinson's

I'm afraid Mr Hall's running a little late, can I get you a tea or coffee while you wait?

No?

What if I tell you about some of the recent cases we've been involved in?

Get comfortable and settle in for a wild ride.

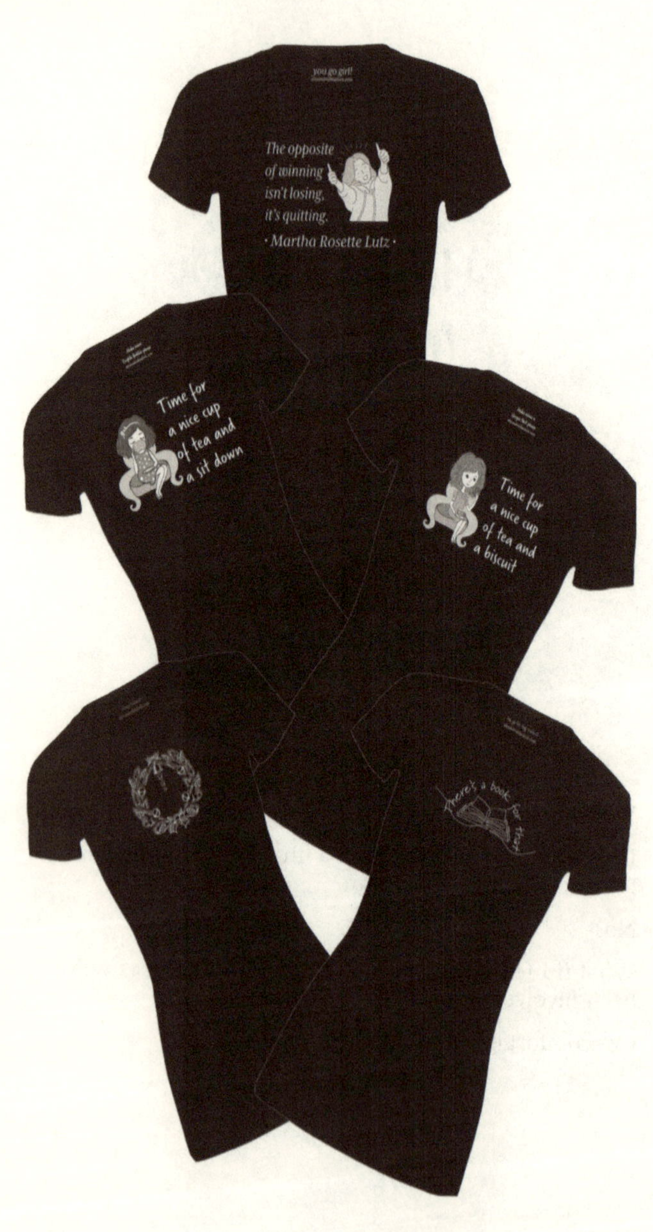
you go girl!
The opposite
of winning
isn't losing,
it's quitting.
· Martha Rosette Lutz ·
Time for
a nice cup
of tea and
a sit down
Time for
a nice cup
of tea and
a biscuit
there's a book for that

Time for a nice cup of tea
and a sit down
BEWARE THE EMPTINESS GREMLINS

Australian author Alexandria Blaelock writes mostly fantasy and mystery.

She's appeared in the Stringybark Anthology *Crowd Surfing*, *Pulphouse Fiction Magazine*, and *Ellery Queen's Mystery Magazine*.

She's also written five self-help books applying business techniques to personal matters like getting dressed, tidying up, and feeding friends.

Discover more at alexandriablaelock.com.

STAY UP TO DATE

Get insider updates on my writing, advance notice of new releases, discounts, free ebooks, stories, and much, much more in my monthly communiqués.

Sign up at

alexandriablaelock.com/insider-updates